This book is dedicated to the Rev. Earle Fox, with admiration, gratitude and love.—E.M.
For Nancy, who would have understood that all the ogre needed was a little love.—E.S.

Copyright © 1991 Rabbit Ears Productions. Inc., Westport, Connecticut.
Rabbit Ears Books is an imprint of Rabbit Ears Productions.
Published by Picture Book Studio Ltd., Saxonville, Massachusetts.
All rights reserved.
Printed in Hong Kong.
10 9 8 7 6 5 4 3 2 1

Library of Congress Cataloging in Publication Data
Metaxas, Eric.
Jack and the beanstalk / retold by Eric Metaxas ; illustrated by Edward Sorel. (We all have tales)
Summary: A boy climbs to the top of a giant beanstalk where he uses his quick wits to outsmart
an ogre and make his and his mother's fortune.
ISBN 0-88708-188-6: $14.95. — ISBN 0-88708-189-4 (book and cassette) : $19.95
[1. Fairy tales. 2. Folklore—England. 3. Giants—Folklore.]
I. Sorel, Edward, 1929- ill. II. Jack and the beanstalk. III. Title. IV. Series.
PZ8.M55Jac 1991
398.2—dc20
[E] 91-14176.

Jack and the Beanstalk

Written by
Eric Metaxas

Illustrated by
Edward Sorel

Rabbit Ears Books

 nce upon a time there lived a poor widow who had an only son named Jack, and an old cow whose name was Milky-White. And all they had to live on was the milk the cow gave them each morning, which they carried to market and sold. But so very exceptional was this milk—for it was far and wide considered the whitest milk anyone had ever seen—that it fetched quite a handsome price at market, and so Jack and his mother were able to get by. 🐮 But alas, one rainy morning, Milky-White gave them no milk. And the next morning Milky-White gave them no milk. And on the morning after that it was precisely the same. Jack and his mother didn't know what to do, and when they spoke to Milky-White herself about it, she was udderly silent. 🐮 "Oh, what shall we do," Jack's mother cried, wringing her hands. "What shall we do?" 🐮 "Cheer up, mother," Jack said bravely. "I'll go out and find some work." 🐮 "No one will hire a boy as young as you are," his mother said. "We have no choice but to sell old Milky-White."

ow, this was the last thing on earth that Jack wanted to do, for he and Milky-White had been the best of friends ever since he could remember. But he knew that there was no other way, and he went outside and took Milky-White by the halter and started off with her down the road to market. He'd not gone far, though, when he came upon a very old, very odd looking man, who tipped his hat and greeted him. "Good morning, Jack," the man said. "Good morning to you," Jack answered, wondering where this strange man had learned his name.

"And where are you off to this bright morning, good Jack?" "I'm going to market to sell our cow," Jack answered, also wondering how this strange man knew that he was good. "Oh, you do look the proper sort of chap to sell cows, don't you? Tell me then, good Jack, if you can, how many beans make five?" "Two in each hand and one in your mouth," Jack answered, just as sharp as a needle.

"And quite right you are, good Jack, quite right you are. And here they are now, the very beans themselves." 🐌 And with a great flourish he pulled out of his tattered waistcoat pocket a number of very strange-looking beans. 🐌 "And as you are so very sharp, good Jack, I don't mind at all making a swap with you—no, not at all, Jack, not in the very least do I mind. What say you then to swapping your old cow there for these extra-ordinary, extravagant, extra-large, extra-extra-extra beans right here." 🐌 And he held them out in the sunlight that Jack might behold them properlike. 🐌 "Oh, go along," Jack said, not to be taken in. "Wouldn't you like it?" 🐌 "Ah," said the man, "but you haven't got the slightest idea as to just what sort of beans these are. By way of illustration, then, I should like to point out that were you to, say, *plant* these beans—oh, in the ground, perhaps—why no sooner than sunup of the following morning would they have grown up into a stalk tall enough to reach the top of the blue sky itself—and not an inch less! Now tell me if *that* doesn't give you pause, tell me."

"Really," said Jack. "You don't say so."

"Oh I most certainly do say so," said the man rather emphatically, "That is precisely and exactly what I say and it is precisely and exactly what would happen—I should stake my very reputation on it."

"But I don't know you," Jack returned. "And what sort of reputation has a stranger got to look out for?" "Oh you are a sharpie, Jack, aren't you? Don't let them tell you otherwise, Jack, any of them, I don't care who they are.

I'll tell you what, if it should happen that anything occurs differently than just as I have described it, in any wise whatever—you can have your cow back. Now there's something, wouldn't you agree?" "Right," says Jack.

And right then and there he handed him over Milky-White's halter and pocketed the five strange-looking beans. Then he bid the strange man a good afternoon and started back home, staring and staring at his wonderful treasure.

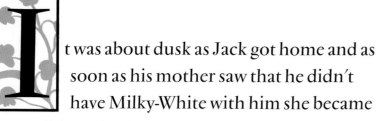

It was about dusk as Jack got home and as soon as his mother saw that he didn't have Milky-White with him she became terribly excited and begged Jack to tell her what price he'd fetched for her. ꙮ "Oh, you'll never guess, mother," Jack said, barely able to contain himself. "Not in a hundred years you won't!" ꙮ "Oh what a good boy you are!" his mother said. "Don't tell me, was it five pounds, or was it... no it couldn't be ten pounds. No? Well it surely couldn't be more than ten pounds. Oh, stop it, Jack, stop it, you must tell me!" ꙮ "There, I told you you couldn't guess," Jack said proudly. "You're not even close, mother, because I didn't get any money for her at all. You see I traded her to an old man for these beans here. He told me that if you plant them they'll grow up to the sky overnight!" ꙮ "Oh my goodness!" said Jack's mother,

putting her hands to her face. "Oh, how could you have been such a fool! Such a dolt! Such an idiot, as to have given away my own Milky-White, the best milker in the parish, and prime beef to boot, for a handful of magical beans!" ꙮ And with that she threw the beans out of the window, and sent him up to bed without so much as a bite of supper. ꙮ Now poor Jack was deeply saddened, and it was not long before he cried himself to sleep, but as he was sleeping he had the strangest dream that ever was. He dreamt that the sun had forgotten to rise one morning and everything in the world became covered in total darkness, and there was a terrific earthquake that split the entire earth quite in two, and when he woke up the chair beside his bed had slid all the way to the other side of the room and there was a strange green hue over everything.

Jack had forgotten the events of the day before, but as soon as he remembered them he leapt to the window and there in all of its splendor he beheld a magnificent beanstalk such as there never has been in the history of the world. It stretched up and up and up—he couldn't see the end of it—and then Jack realized that it stretched up beyond the blue circle of the sky itself, just as the strange man had predicted. And so, without a moment's hesitation, Jack leapt out of his window, onto the beanstalk, and began climbing. And he climbed, and he climbed, and he climbed, and he climbed, and he climbed, until at last he was able to touch the surface of the blue sky itself, and he poked his head through it, and there, just on the other side, he saw a road stretching off into the distance. So Jack pulled himself over the edge of the sky and started down the road, thinking of nothing but where he could find some breakfast, for it had been an awfully long climb and, as you will no doubt remember, he hadn't eaten a crumb since the morning of the day before.

ow the countryside all around him was unlike anything he'd ever seen—everything was larger and wilder than what he was used to—and his prospects for finding breakfast seemed, on the whole, rather dim. Then he came upon a great big tall house, larger than any he'd ever seen, and on the doorstep there stood a great big tall woman. "Good morning, mum," said Jack, quite polite-like, for he was as hungry as a hunter. "Could you be so kind as to give me some breakfast?" "There now, you'd better be running along, for I am married to an ogre and there isn't a thing he prefers for his breakfast to broiled English boys on toast.

Run along then." But Jack's hunger had quite a strong grip on him and he pleaded: "Please, mum. I've had nothing to eat since yesterday morning. I may just as well take my chances being eaten by an ogre as die of hunger." "Well," said the ogre's wife, "that's certainly reasonable enough then, isn't it?" So, she took Jack into the kitchen and gave him a chunk of black bread and a chunk of yellow cheese and a jug of white milk, although Jack couldn't help noticing how very much whiter Milky-White's milk had always been.

ack had barely finished eating when he heard a **THUMP! THUMP! THUMP!** coming through the house that scared him mostly out of wits. "Goodness gracious," she said. "My husband is coming! What shall I do? Quick, hop in here." And she scooped Jack into the oven just as the ogre came into the room The ogre was a wild, smelly man, and a large one at that. And Jack saw that as he came into the room he carried the body of a cow slung over his shoulder, which he threw on the floor roughly. "Here, wife. Broil this for my breakfast. Ah! What's that

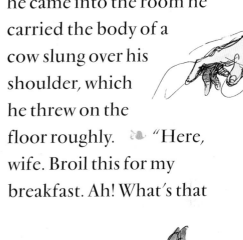

I smell?" he inquired. *"Fee-Fie-Foe-Fum, I smell the blood of an Englishman! Be he live or be he dead, I'll have his bones to grind my bread!"* "Nonsense, dearie," his wife said cheerfully. "You must be dreaming. Unless, of course, it's the scraps of that English boy you had for yesterday's dinner. Off you go and have a scrub-up and tidy yourself and by the time you come back your breakfast will be ready."

So off the ogre went, and Jack was just about to jump out of the oven when the woman pushed him back in. "Wait till he's asleep," said she with a wink. "He always has a doze after his breakfast."

ell, the ogre returned and ate his breakfast. He burped very, very loudly, sending such an awful stench through the room that Jack thought he would faint dead right then and there in the oven and be discovered. 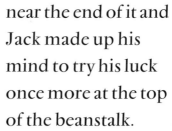 After that the ogre went to a huge chest and took out a couple of bags of gold, which he sat down and counted, until at last his head began to nod and he fell asleep. He began to snore till the whole house shook again. Then Jack crept out on tiptoe from the oven and as he was passing the ogre he slipped one of the bags of gold under his arm. Then he ran out of the door, and down the long road until he saw the top of the beanstalk sticking

up through the sky. When he reached it he threw the bag of gold down, which made a hole six feet deep in his mother's garden, and began the long, long climb back home. When he reached the bottom his mother had just fished the bag of gold out of from the hole it had made in her garden. "Well, mother," Jack said proudly, "wasn't I right about those beans. They really did grow, didn't they?" And as she agreed, she and Jack danced merrily around the bottom of the beanstalk, for she'd never been as happy in all her life. And so they lived off the bag of gold for some time, but at last they came near the end of it and Jack made up his mind to try his luck once more at the top of the beanstalk.

o very early one morning, he climbed out of his window onto the beanstalk and started climbing. And he climbed and he climbed and he climbed and he climbed and he climbed until...and he climbed and he climbed and he climbed...until at last he came to the end of it and pulled himself up over the blue sky and started down the road again. And before too long he came to the same great big house and before it stood the same great big tall woman on the doorstep. 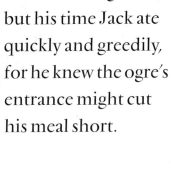 "Good morning, mum," Jack said, as bold as brass. "Could you be so good as to give me something to eat?" 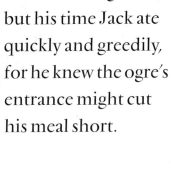 "Say there," said the woman, "aren't you the very lad who

came here once before? My husband lost one of his bags of gold on the very day you were here. You'd better be running along now before he kills you dead and scrambles you into his eggs and eats you." 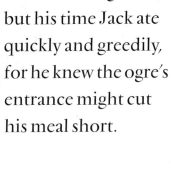 "Now that's odd, mum," Jack replied. "Bag of gold, eh? I dare say it has a familiar ring to it, but I could never remember anything too well before breakfast. It's just tragical trying to think on an empty stomach, mum—just tragical, that's what it is." 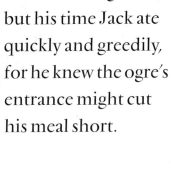 Well, the big woman was so curious that she took him into the kitchen and gave him something to eat, but his time Jack ate quickly and greedily, for he knew the ogre's entrance might cut his meal short.

And sure enough, no sooner had he his last bite than **THUMP! THUMP! THUMP!** he heard the giant's footsteps, and the big woman hid Jack away in the oven just as before. And everything else happened just as before. 🐚 In came the ogre just as before and just as before he said: *"Fee-Fie-Foe-Fum,"* and dumped the cow onto the floor and the ogre's wife cooked it up and the ogre ate it up for breakfast and when he was quite full he let fly another burp so horrible that it made the first one smell like a petunia in comparison, and Jack thought he might very well scream and give himself away. 🐚 Then the ogre said: "Wife, bring me that hen that lays the golden eggs." 🐚 And so she brought it in and placed it on the table before him and the ogre said to it: 🐚 "Lay!" 🐚 The hen shook her feathers and walked in a small circle on the table and then she sat down and without the slightest ado she laid a handsome egg of the purest gold. The ogre's head began to nod and he fell asleep. And just as before he began to snore so loudly the whole house shook. 🐚 As he saw this, Jack crept out of the oven and stole over to where the golden hen was, and before you could say "Jack Robinson" he was off.

ut this time around the hen gave out a little cackle of gratitude that woke the ogre, and just as Jack was climbing over the doorstep he heard the ogre calling: "Wife, wife, what have you done with my golden egg?" And the wife said: "Why, my dear?" But that was all Jack was able to hear, for he rushed like a madman down the road to the waiting beanstalk and climbed down with all the frenzy of a house on fire. And when he got home he showed his mother the wonderful hen and placed it on the table and said to it: "Lay!" And every time he said this to it, it turned a small circle and then laid a perfect egg, just as simple as you please. Well, Jack was not the sort to be content for very long, and it wasn't a month before he decided to have another try at his luck at the top of the beanstalk. So very, very early one morning, Jack got out of bed, walked to his window and jumped onto the beanstalk. And he climbed and he climbed and he climbed and he climbed and he climbed...and he climbed and he climbed and he...climbed and he climbed... until at last he came to the top of the beanstalk and he lifted himself up over the edge of the blue sky and started down the road to the ogre's house.

ut this time he knew better than to go to the doorstep, so he waited behind a bush until he saw the ogre's wife come out with a pail to get water and then he crept into the house and hid inside the large copper broiler. 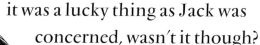 And he hadn't been there long when he heard **THUMP! THUMP! THUMP!** and just as before, in came the ogre and his wife. *"Fee-Fie-Foe-Fum, I smell the blood of an Englishman,"* cried the ogre. "I smell him, wife, I smell him." "Do you, my dumpling," said the ogre's wife. "Well, if it's that little rogue that stole your gold and the hen that lays the golden eggs, he's sure to be hiding in the oven." And they both rushed to the oven and threw

open the door, but Jack wasn't there at all and the ogre's wife said: "There you are again with your *Fee-Fie-Foe-Fum*. Why it must be that other boy that I cooked up last night that you're smelling, of course it is. How forgetful I am, and how careless you are not to know the difference between what's live and what's dead." So the ogre sat down to his horrible breakfast and began eating, but every now and then he'd mutter: "Well, I could have sworn..." And then he'd get up and search the larder and the cupboards and everything, only he didn't think of searching the copper broiler, and it was a lucky thing as Jack was concerned, wasn't it though?

Just after breakfast the ogre called out: 🐚 "Wife, Wife, bring me my golden harp." 🐚 So she brought it and put it on the table in front before him. 🐚 Then he said: "Sing!" 🐚 And the harp sang so beautifully that Jack almost poked his head out from the broiler to see it, but he knew that he must wait until the ogre was asleep, and sure enough the ogre soon fell asleep and began to snore like thunder. 🐚 Then Jack lifted up the broiler lid very quietly and got down like a mouse and crept on his hands and knees till he came to the table. Then up he crawled, caught hold of the golden harp and made a dash for the door. But even before he reached the door the harp called

out: 🐚 "Master! Master!" 🐚 The ogre woke up just in time to see Jack running off with his harp. 🐚 Jack ran as fast as he could, and the ogre came rushing after him. He would easily have caught him, but Jack had a head start and dodged him a bit and knew just where he was going. 🐚 When he finally got to the beanstalk the ogre was less than twenty yards away. Then the ogre saw Jack suddenly disappear, and when he got to the end of the road he saw Jack climbing down the beanstalk for his dear life. 🐚 Well, the ogre didn't think the beanstalk would hold his weight, so for a moment he just stood there and watched, but then the harp cried out again: 🐚 Master! Master!"

And without thinking the ogre swung himself down onto the beanstalk, which shook with his weight. Down, down, down climbed Jack, faster than he'd ever gone before, and after him climbed the ogre.

☙ But this time, when he was about a hundred meters up Jack saw his mother in the garden chopping wood and he called out to her: ☙ "Mother! Mother! Come quickly and bring me the axe!" ☙ And his mother came rushing over to the beanstalk and looked up and stood frozen with fright, for the ogre's legs had just appeared through the clouds and he was descending rather quickly. But Jack soon jumped down and grabbed the axe and started chopping away at the beanstalk with every bit of his strength.

☙ Now the ogre felt the beanstalk shaking, so he stopped to see what was the matter, which wasn't the thing to do just then, as Jack gave the beanstalk another splendid chop and it began to give way. And it was just then that the ogre lost his grip and began to fall from the sky.

End over end over end he fell, until at last he hit the earth and broke his crown, and not very far from where Jack and his mother were standing, and the beanstalk toppled after him. The celebration was quite a large one, and Jack showed his mother the golden harp. After he sold all the golden eggs the hen had laid, Jack and his mother became very rich and he married a great princess and they lived very, very, very happily ever after.